For Tom and Catherine – our treasure
EG

To Mama and Papa
JT

First published 2017 by Nosy Crow Ltd
The Crow's Nest, 14 Baden Place, Crosby Row
London, SE1 1YW, UK
www.nosycrow.com

ISBN 978 0 85763 889 2 (HB)
ISBN 978 0 85763 890 8 (PB)

Nosy Crow and associated logos are trademarks and/or registered trademarks of Nosy Crow Ltd.

Text © Mal Peet and Elspeth Graham 2017
Illustrations © Jez Tuya 2017

The right of Mal Peet and Elspeth Graham to be identified as the authors and
of Jez Tuya to be identified as the illustrator of this work has been asserted.

A CIP catalogue record for this book is available from the British Library.

Printed in Turkey by Imago.

Papers used by Nosy Crow are made from wood grown in sustainable forests.

1 3 5 7 9 8 6 4 2 (HB)
3 5 7 9 8 6 4 2 (PB)

The Treasure of Pirate Frank

Mal Peet and
Elspeth Graham

Jez Tuya

nosy
crow

This is the boy who wants to find
the treasure of Pirate Frank.

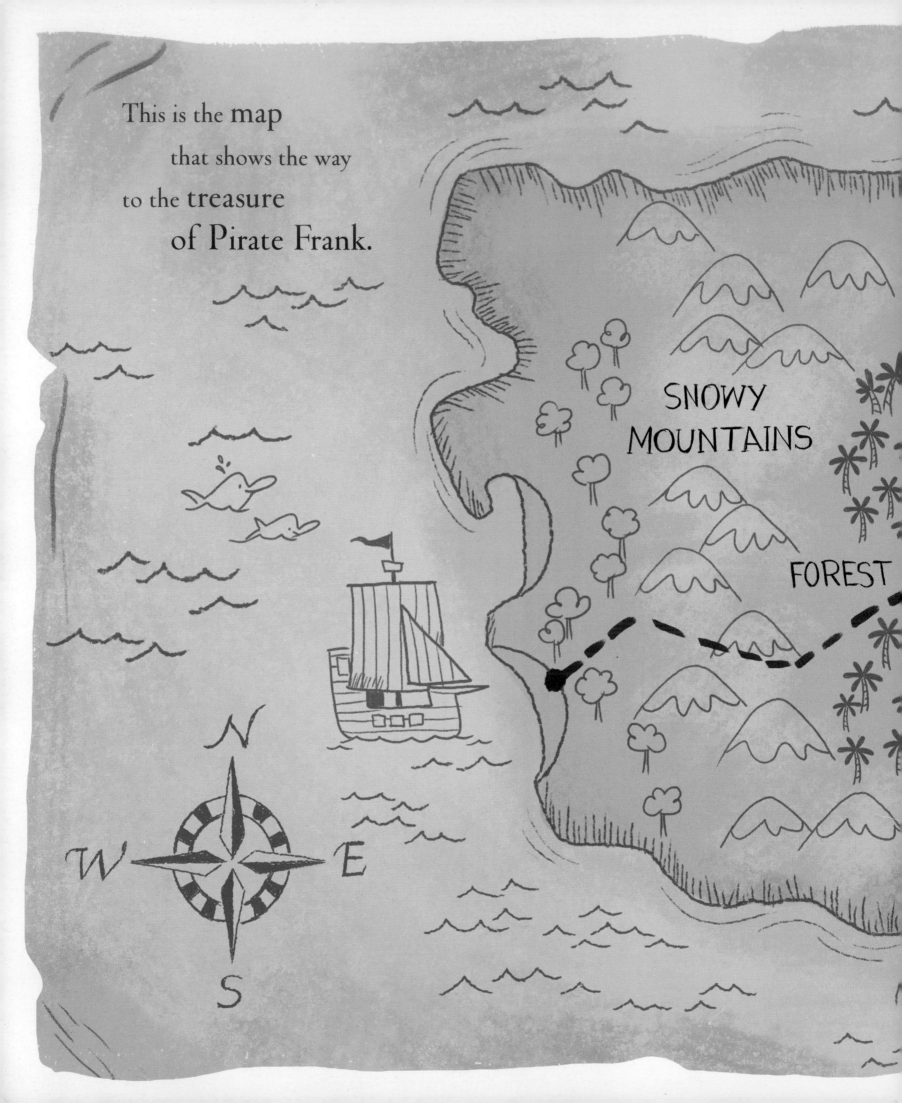

This is the **map**
that shows the way
to the **treasure**
of Pirate Frank.

SNOWY
MOUNTAINS

FOREST

N
W   E
S

This is the **sea** that must be sailed.

It's on the **map** that shows the way
to the **treasure of Pirate Frank**.

There's the **island** of spice and gold
beyond the **sea** that must be sailed.

It's on the **map** that shows the way
to the **treasure of Pirate Frank.**

These are the **mountains** snowy and cold

on the **island** of spice and gold

beyond the **sea** that must be sailed.

They're on the **map** that shows the way
to the **treasure of Pirate Frank.**

Here's the forest where monkeys swing
over the mountains snowy and cold
on the island of spice and gold
beyond the sea that must be sailed.

It's on the **map** that shows the way
to the **treasure** of Pirate Frank.

This is the **swamp** where bullfrogs sing
past the **forest** where monkeys swing
over the **mountains** snowy and cold
on the **island** of spice and gold
beyond the **sea** that must be sailed.

It's on the **map**
that shows the way
to the **treasure**
of Pirate Frank.

Here are the steps going higher and higher
above the swamp where bullfrogs sing
past the forest where monkeys swing
over the mountains snowy and cold
on the island of spice and gold
beyond the sea that must be sailed.

They're on the **map** that shows the way
to the **treasure of Pirate Frank.**

Here's the volcano that spits out fire
at the top of the steps going higher and higher
above the swamp where bullfrogs sing
past the forest where monkeys swing
over the mountains snowy and cold
on the island of spice and gold
beyond the sea that must be sailed.

It's on the **map** that shows the way
to the **treasure of Pirate Frank.**

There's the tall **tree** that marks the spot
beside the **volcano** that spits out fire
at the top of the **steps** going higher and higher
above the **swamp** where bullfrogs sing
past the **forest** where monkeys swing
over the **mountains** snowy and cold
on the **island** of spice and gold
beyond the **sea** that must be sailed.

It's on the **map** that shows the way
to the **treasure** of Pirate Frank.

And under the **tree** that marks the spot is . . .

. . . Pirate Frank!

She's not on the map!

Quick! Run!
Down the **steps**
going lower, not higher,
below the **volcano**
that spits out fire . . .

through the **swamp**
where bullfrogs sing . . .

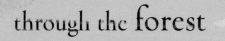

through the forest
where monkeys swing . . .

over the mountains
snowy and cold . . .

. . . and off the **island**
of spice and gold,
into the ship, to sail away . . .

. . . and dream of what was found today . . .

. . . the treasure of Pirate Frank.